...while Dora loves to EAT!

Sid runs a busy restaurant.
There's lots of food to try,

Usborne Dinosaur Tales

The Dinosaur Who Roared For MORE

Russell Punter

Illustrated by Andy Elkerton

Reading consultant: Alison Kelly

Down in Dino Valley, there are lots of friends to meet.

Here's Sid at work.
He loves to cook...

from steaming
soup,

and veggie
stew,

to smooth
banoffee pie.

Most customers don't eat too much.

They start with something small...

a main course...

then a
fruit
dessert.

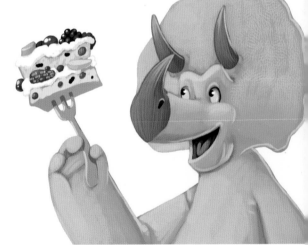

"We're all full now,"
they call.

Then one day,
Dora waddles in.

She just can't wait to eat.

Sid rushes up to
welcome her...

and shows her to a seat.

He hands her a long menu.
"What would you like
to start?"

Dora grins and licks her lips. "I'll try the mushroom tart."

Minutes later, Sid returns.

"You'll love this dish,
I'm sure."

Dora chomps the tart
down fast...

and then she roars for...

MORE!

Sid rustles up another tart.

It goes down like before.

Sid reaches out to take the plate and Dora roars for...

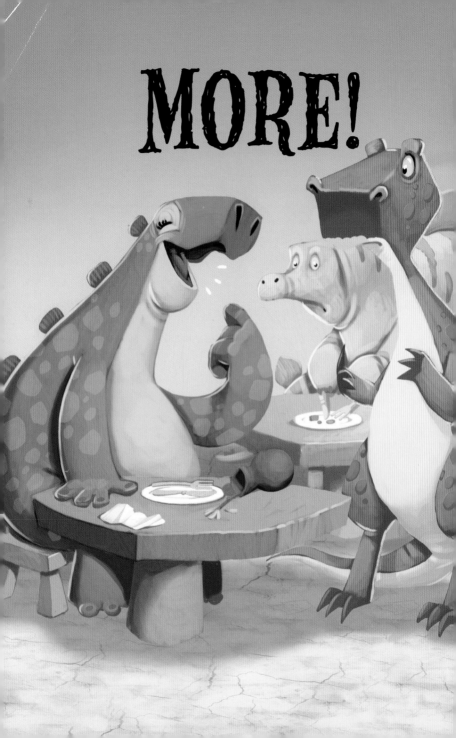

Dora eats
tart number
three...

then
number
four...

and five.

"My main course, then.
I'll try the rich fish pie."

Minutes later, Sid returns.

"You'll love this dish,
I'm sure."

Dora gobbles up the pie...

and then she roars for...

MORE!

Sid prepares another pie.

It goes down like before.

Sid reaches out to take the plate and Dora roars for...

MORE!

Pie number three,

then four,

then five,
all vanish from
her plate.

There goes
six,

soon seven's gone,

and so has
number eight.

"Please bring dessert. My tummy mustn't rumble!"

Sid brings her order
out at once.

"One toffee
apple crumble."

She guzzles up the crumble fast, as custard hits the floor.

"That was yummy," she declares, but then she roars for...

MORE!

Sid brings another crumble.
It goes down like before.

Sid reaches out to take the
bowl and Dora roars for...

MORE!

Crumble number three goes down...

then four...

five,
six

and seven.

Then number eight...

and
nine...

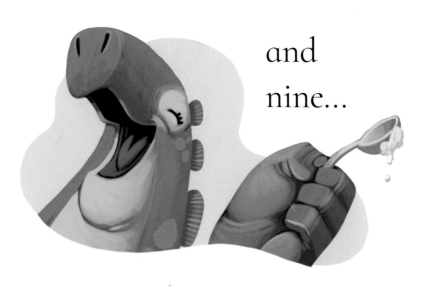

and ten.

Says Dora,
"This is
heaven!"

BURP!

"That should be fine
till supper time...

I may be back for more."
But when she leaves,
to head for home...

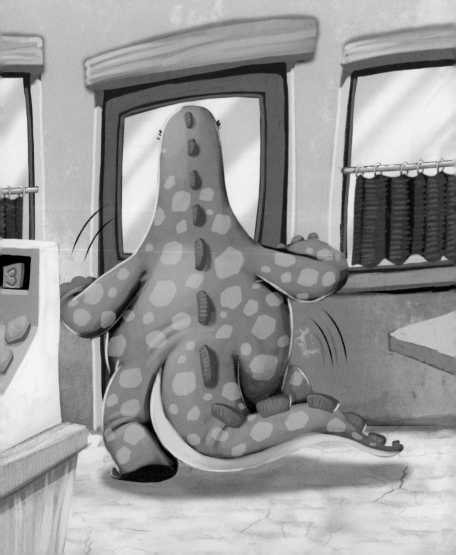

She can't fit
through the door!

Sid tries to help.

He bumps...

and shoves...

but he can't move poor Dora.

"You've eaten too much food," he pants.

"Stay here till you get smaller."

So Dora helps Sid serve his food.

She's on her feet all day.

She huffs and puffs and
pants at first.

But soon she feels okay.

One week later, Dora's off.
She fits right through
the door.

"I liked working here,"
she says. "I'd like to work
some more."

Now Dora has fun
helping out.

She skips across the floor.

She eats good food,
but not too much...

and never roars for more!

Series editor: Lesley Sims

First published in 2020 by Usborne Publishing Ltd., Usborne House,
83-85 Saffron Hill, London EC1N 8RT, England. usborne.com
Copyright © 2020 Usborne Publishing Ltd.

USBORNE FIRST READING
Level Four

Little Red Riding Hood

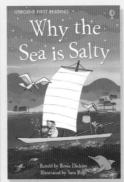

Why the Sea is Salty

The Hare and the Tortoise

The Emperor and the Nightingale

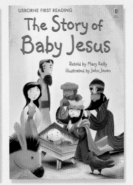

The Story of Baby Jesus

The Three Wishes

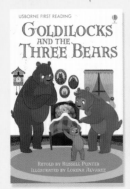

Goldilocks and the Three Bears

The Golden Carpet

Androcles and the Lion